Be the Vet

7 Dog + Cat Stories

Test Your Veterinary Knowledge

Volume 2

By: Dr. Ed Blesy and Marcy Blesy

Follow our *Be the Vet* Facebook page for more specific information.

Introduction

In *Be the Vet*, you will learn diagnoses for common veterinary problems. First you will read a story about a family with a dog or cat. The animal will experience a health issue, sometimes the result of an illness and sometimes the result of an emergency. You will have the opportunity to make your own notes as if you were the veterinarian diagnosing the problem and make a diagnostic plan, or treatment plan, to help the pet. Using a notebook or piece of paper, you will write down the pet's symptoms and the steps you would go through to assess the problem followed by your suggestions for treatment.

For example:

Name of the Animal (patient): Fido

Type of Animal: Dog

Symptoms or Injuries: Not eating, Difficulty walking, etc.

Treatment: Do blood work. Give medication. Take X-rays, etc.

Then you will compare your plan with that of Dr. Edmund Blesy, a licensed veterinarian with sixteen years of experience in veterinary practice. Dr. Blesy will go into more detail than you will, but writing down what you know from the story paired with your own ideas will help you learn to think like a doctor.

The diagnoses given in this book are specific to the fictional cases presented. Should your pet experience health problems, please consult your own veterinarian as each case is unique and needs its own analysis. The cases in this book are meant to give general information and educate the reader about common veterinary problems.

Table of Contents

Lethargic

I can't believe it's finally here—warm weather. We've had snow from October to April even though spring started a few weeks ago. I mean, how are we supposed to use up our energy if we can't run around outside? And who wants to run around outside in the cold? Don't get me wrong. The snow was fun…at first, but by the tenth snow day off from school, I'd had enough. We already have to go to school three extra days in June now.

Anyway, I'm just glad that today is here. It's seventy degrees outside, and Mom and Dad are taking me to the beach. Of course, the lake water is still cold, but we'll run around on the sand dunes with our dog Freckles. Then we will look for beach glass along the water. Beach glass is really just broken bottle pieces, but from all the churning and pounding in the water they receive, the sharp edges are dulled into cool shapes of glass to collect.

"Load Freckles in the car," yells Mom from downstairs. "And grab her leash." I hunt for Freckle's pink leash. Dogs aren't allowed to run free at the beach, though

Freckles would love nothing more than to fetch sticks thrown into the water or race ahead of us on the trail.

Freckle's tail keeps smacking me against my face in the backseat of the car. She's a big dog, even for a Golden Retriever. I know she knows our agenda for this trip. It's been a long winter for her, too.

"Do you want to walk on the beach first or take a hike along the trail?" asks Dad.

"Let's take the trail first. That way we don't have to carry all of our beach glass with us," I say.

Mom laughs. "Do you really think we'll find that much glass?" she asks.

"Duh, Mom. Nobody has better beach glass spotting eyes that me."

She shakes her head and laughs again. "We'll see," she says.

When we get to the start of the trail, I hand Freckle's leash to Dad. Running ahead of my parents, I stop only to jump over fallen logs or slide down mounds of loose sand. Next year I'm joining the track team. I need some real competition. My parents do *not* qualify. I'm about to exit the trail in the dunes and head to the beach when I hear branches breaking and barking coming from behind. I turn around and see Freckles barreling toward me, her leash flying in the wind behind her. Dad is hollering somewhere far back on the trail. I reach out and grab hold of the pink leash just before Freckles takes off after a little dog that is yapping down on the beach.

"I have Freckles!" I yell to my parents. They are both out of breath when they get to me. No, my parents are definitely not competition when it comes to running.

"I guess someone else is tired of being cooped up inside, too," says Mom. "Take Freckles to the beach, but head down there," Mom says, pointing to a sandy trail through the tall, beach grass. "We don't need that little dog nipping at her."

I tighten my grip on the leash and let Freckles lead me toward the beach with a few jerks of the leash away from the little dog. The sun feels so good. It's amazing what a little fresh air will do to my mood, too. I doubt anything could spoil this day. Spotting my first piece of beach glass for the season confirms what I thought this day would be like. It's a deep blue color. The sun reflecting off its surface looks like a thousand twinkling stars on a clear night. Freckles stops to drink from the lake when I bend down to pick up another piece of glass, this one a clear glass color. Freckles greets me with a kiss before I can stand up straight.

"Gross! Cut it out, Freckles." She nudges her head against my leg in an apology of sorts. I sit on the warm sand and kick off my shoes. Freckles lies down next to me. As I'm petting her thick fur, not yet thinned from her winter coat, I feel something. I think it's a burr, a sticky pricker from a bush along the dune trail. I look closer and notice at least five more prickers, only I'm not so sure that's what they are. They look more like bugs. I wave over my parents who are sitting on a piece of driftwood, a few feet away.

"What's up?" asks Dad.

"Look at Freckles." I point to the bugs attached to her coat.

Dad takes one look and makes his diagnoses. "Ticks," he says. "We have to get them off." He pulls off the bugs with his fingers. Then he starts combing through Freckle's hair. "There's a couple more on her skin."

"Under her fur?" I ask.

He shakes his head *yes*.

"Is that bad?"

"I think it could be. The ticks on her skin are attached more firmly, and I don't have anything to pull them off with. Let's go home to get some tweezers."

"Will Freckles be okay?" I ask.

"I think so. The dunes are crawling with ticks. We just have to be careful and check all of us out, too."

*****

Three Months Later…

The first day of summer vacation is tomorrow. I can't wait for a long break from school. The last couple of months have been crazy busy with soccer games, variety show practices, and, of course, lots of visits to the beach.

My parents have been letting me run down to the beach with Freckles as long as I take along another friend. There isn't near as much beach glass as there was when we started coming back to the beach in early spring. Lots of other people comb the beach during the day, and the pickings are slim by the time I get down here. Once school's out I'll be one of the first people at the beach in the morning. I'll even set my alarm if I have to. Finding a red piece of glass is my goal for the summer.

I grab Freckle's leash from the hook by the back door. "Mom, I'm meeting Jordan at the corner, and we're running down to the beach."

"Sounds good. Bring your phone."

I call for the dog, but she doesn't come. That's weird. She loves her runs to the beach. I hunt for Freckles in her usual spot, the screened-in back porch, bathed in a patch of sun. She's not there. I put down the leash and search the house. After a few minutes, I find Freckles under the kitchen table. Her front paw is over her face. I swear if a dog could look depressed, that would describe Freckles. I call to her, but she barely lifts her head. I try to coax her out with a treat from the kitchen pantry. That doesn't work, either, which is *really* weird.

"Mom, come here!" Mom and I try to move Freckles out from under the table. She gets up but falls back to the ground right away. We try again. This time she walks, but her front paw seems to give out as she stumbles forward. She looks dazed and weak. I look at Mom. She takes a deep breath and lets out a sigh.

"Get a blanket for Freckles. She feels warm. Stay with her a minute. I'm going to call the veterinarian," she says.

*****

If you were the veterinarian, what would you do next? Make a list of Freckle's injuries. Then make a diagnostic (treatment) plan based upon the information that you have. When you are done, read what the veterinarian will do.

Name of the Animal (patient):

Type of Animal:

Symptoms or Injuries:

Treatment:

History:

*Freckles is lethargic. In other words, she is not as active as usual.

*Freckles is weak and has trouble walking.

*There has been no known trauma. For example, Freckles did not fall or get hit by a car.

*Her weakened condition appeared to develop quickly.

Assessment:

*First assess Freckles' general condition.

*There are no apparent signs of trauma. Freckles is not bleeding and has no bruising.

*Multiple limbs are weak. Freckles is unable to put much weight on a front and a back leg.

Paresis: Muscle weakness caused by nerve damage or disease.

*Check her mucous membrane color (the tissue in the gums of her mouth). The fact that Freckles has pink mucous membranes can help rule out other causes of weakness.

*The temperature is elevated at 103.6 degrees.

*Normal temperature of dogs is 99.5-102.5 degrees. Dog and cats have a body temperature that is naturally higher than humans. You should have a temperature between 97.6 and 99.6 degrees.

*"The technician took the temperature from the bottom!" Veterinarians will often take a rectal temperature. This method is still considered the most accurate way to measure the body temperature of pets. Please do not attempt to take the temperature of your pet at home without the guidance of an adult. Injury can occur if this is not done properly.

The veterinarian decides to run laboratory tests on a blood sample.

*CBC Test: This stands for complete blood count. Types of blood cell numbers, which include red and white, can give veterinarians clues to an animal's overall health.

*Blood Chemistry Test: This test measures a variety of substances in the blood. Examples are proteins and enzymes. This test can be used to scan for things that may have caused weakness.

*Lyme Test: This is a specific lab test to see if Freckles has been exposed to the bacteria that causes Lyme disease.

Diagnosis: Lyme disease

*The Lyme test is positive. The CBC and blood chemistry does not show any other problems.

Treatment Plan:

*Freckles is sent home with antibiotics to treat Lyme disease.

*Lyme disease is caused by a type of bacteria. Bacteria are very small living organisms that can be found everywhere.

*Antibiotics are medicine that can cure disease caused by bacteria. They do not work against viruses.

*The bacteria were injected into Freckles when a tick was attached and feeding off the blood of Freckles.

*Not all types of ticks carry the bacteria that cause Lyme disease.

*The veterinary team will recommend a good tick preventative to lessen the risk of tick attachment to Freckles. A tick preventative is a type of medication either applied to the skin, given orally, or on a special collar.

TICK AND LYME FACTS:

*One tick can lay thousands of eggs.

*The blacklegged tick, or deer tick, is the species of tick that carries the Lyme bacteria. A stage of the tick called the nymph stage is responsible for transmitting the majority of the cases of Lyme disease. The nymph is less than 2mm in size. (This is not much more than a tip of a pen!)

*To prevent transmission of disease-causing organisms to pets and to humans, remove ticks with fine-toothed tweezers. Get close to the skin and pull straight out. **DO NOT use soap, Vaseline, a match head, etc. to remove a tick.** These techniques may work to get the tick to back out, but there is more chance for bacteria to be regurgitated or injected into the host by the tick.

*If the head or mouth parts of the tick remain, leave them alone. The skin should heal.

*Dogs are more resistant than people to the disease. Cats are more resistant than dogs. Less than 10% of dogs that get exposed to the bacteria will ever show signs.

*Additional protection from Lyme disease in the form of a vaccine is available for dogs.

*Visit the CDC (Centers for Disease Control and Prevention) website for the latest information on Lyme disease.

*****

Freckles responds quickly to the antibiotics. Thank goodness. She is acting a lot more like herself. She still likes to take long walks and runs into the lake to take a bath. We are very careful when we take Freckles to the dunes or anywhere that has tall grass. We even check her fur after she's been in the backyard for a while because we have learned that ticks can be just about anywhere in nature. It's scary to think that Freckles could have another Lyme-infested tick stick into her skin. However, now we know what to look for on her *and* on us because people can get Lyme disease, too. And just the other day, when I was about to head home after a long walk with Freckles on the beach, guess what I found, right in front of Freckles? Reflecting the rays of the sun as if to call me by name—a beautiful piece of rare, red beach glass waited for me to scoop it up. The summer is looking up—for Freckles *and* me.

Itchy

Vacuum the living room. Sweep the laundry room. Scoop the litter box. All of these commands from my mom ring through my head as I make a mental checklist so that I can tick them off one by one when I complete the assigned tasks. Mom's usually not this bad, but with my older sister's high school graduation party coming up and a hundred people coming to our house in two days, she's a little frantic. Dad's not better *Mow the backyard. Pull the weeds in the garden. Wash the car.* I highly doubt any guests at the graduation party are going to care if the car in the garage is washed or not. In fact, the car will likely be parked at the neighbor's house anyway to make use of the garage space for tables and chairs. That's my sister's job, though, setting up all the stuff needed to feed these people and keep them happy. Since Mom and Dad work full-time jobs, they've really been relying on us since we're done with school for the summer. I'd rather be reading or surfing the internet or swimming at my best friend's house, but since this only happens once in a lifetime (well, twice if you count *my* future graduation), then I can take it.

When I start the vacuum, our cat Doc darts out of the room and through the cat door down to the basement. He's always hated the vacuum. I suppose if I was a foot tall, the rumblings of the vacuum might send terror rushing through my veins, too. I honestly don't know why I'm vacuuming now when I'll just have to do it again the morning of the party. Doc sheds his black and white fur so badly that an hour later the carpet will look exactly the same as it does now—tufts of fur scattered about like tumbleweeds rolling over our floor.

I'm enjoying a glass of lemonade on the back deck when I hear my mom hollering. My sister and I give each other an *oh brother, what now?* look.

"Coming, Mom!" we yell in unison. She's standing in the living room pointing to a new pile of Doc's fur.

"I thought I told you to vacuum," she says.

"I did!"

"Well, it certainly doesn't look like it," she says. I sigh and scrunch up my face so I don't say something I regret. She notices.

"Look, I'm sorry it seems like I'm being really hard on you guys, but there are a lot of people coming soon, and I don't think…"

My sister puts her hand on Mom's arm. "It's all going to be okay," she says. "The party will be perfect."

Mom gives the tiniest hint of a smile and nods her head. That's when we hear a strange scratching sound coming from behind us in the kitchen. "What on earth?" says Mom.

We turn around and see Doc sitting on the kitchen floor pawing at his ear, and not the *lick, lick, clean my ear* kind of pawing, either. He's scratching like he's in pain. I can empathize. I once had a mosquito bite on the back of my ankle that hurt so bad I did just about anything to make it stop itching. I rubbed it raw until it bled. Leaning over Doc, I take a closer look. In addition to the fur flying around in the air, there are specks of blood around the outside of the right ear. I don't know if something bit Doc and made him bleed or if his own claws cut his ear with the itching. That's what I suspect.

"Mom, his ear is bleeding," I say.

"Put him in his carrier, and I'll call the vet," she says.

Doc shakes his head adamantly like he's protesting the visit to the vet, sending more fur into the air. Poor guy. I pet Doc before subjecting him to the cat carrier, which he hates. His ear looks dirty and raw from all the rubbing. I sure hope the vet can figure this out in time for my sister's party, for the sake of Doc *and* my mom's sanity!

*****

If you were the veterinarian, what would you do next? Make a list of Doc's injuries. Then make a diagnostic (treatment) plan based upon the information that you have. When you are done, read what the veterinarian will do.

Name of the Animal (patient):

Type of Animal:

Symptoms or Injuries:

Treatment:

History:

*The owner noticed Doc digging aggressively at his ears.

*The owner also noticed a bleeding skin lesion.

*The veterinarian or veterinarian technician may ask the owner various questions. The answers will help with assessing the animal's illness and possibly with treatment decisions. In Doc's case, the techs want to know if Doc ever went outside or was around other cats and dogs. The answer was *yes*. Doc has gotten outside multiple times.

Assessment:

*Doc has sores on his head at the base of the ears.

*There is also a large amount of dark debris (gunk) in both ears.

*Ear mites are suspected, but this should be confirmed with testing.

NOTE: Do not assume all cats and dogs with dark ear debris have ear mites. Dark debris may also indicate infection with bacteria or yeast.

*An otoscope can be used to see tiny moving organisms within the ear canal. An otoscope is a medical instrument with a light and magnification used to inspect the ear. This means this instrument has the ability to help the veterinarian see small things inside the ear canal.

*If the veterinarian cannot see any mites with the otoscope, some of the debris can be removed from the ear canal with cotton swabs for inspection. The material is put on a slide and examined under a microscope. A microscope is a lab instrument used for viewing very small objects.

Treatment Plan:

*The veterinary technician applies a solution to Doc's ears. This one time treatment will kill the ear mites.

NOTE: There are various labeled products to treat ear mites. Some must be used for numerous days, and are, therefore, inconvenient treatments. The veterinarian will help an owner choose the easiest and most effective treatment.

Question: During the assessment of the patient by the veterinarian, she learns that Doc has gone outside. Why is this information important?

*This explains how Doc acquired ear mites. It takes contact with another dog or cat to get ear mites.

*If Doc has been outside, there is increased risk for Doc to get other parasites. This includes fleas and heartworms. The veterinary staff can recommend products to protect Doc.

*Doc has more chance of getting a disease from other outdoor cats. Therefore, the veterinarian will make different vaccine recommendations to protect Doc.

FACT:

*Ear mites pass easily from pet to pet. Therefore, all pets in a home must be treated to get rid of the mites.

*Humans are extremely unlikely to be affected by ear mites.

*Rabbits and ferrets can also get the mites.

*****

"I think that's the last load of garbage," I say to Mom. I lug the heavy plastic bag over my shoulder and dump it into the outside trash can. "It's a miracle we have any room left in here," I say, pointing to the garbage can.

"It's actually our second can of trash," says Mom. "The neighbors lent us their can earlier."

I laugh. "Good planning, Mom."

My sister puts her arm around Mom's shoulders. "See, Mom, I told you everything would be okay. My graduation party was a huge success."

"And Doc is on the mend," I add.

Mom has tears in her eyes. I think seeing her oldest daughter graduate high school has been hard on her. "Speaking of Doc," she says. "I think we are overdue for a long nap."

"Good plan, Mom. I'm sure Doc has already gotten a head start."

There is not a much better way to spend a summer day than to nap in a warm patch of sun.

Storm

Sunny sprints around the backyard fetching the new ball we just bought at the pet supply store. It's the first time our new puppy went shopping with us. I insisted that she pick out her own ball. My older brother said I was being ridiculous, that how in the world would a dog know what kind of ball she'd like better over another, but I told him *he* was the ridiculous one because how would he like it if Mom picked out all of his clothes? Maybe Mom should try that just so my brother can see what it's like not to have any control over his own life. Anyway, Sunny knew exactly what she wanted when she parked herself in front of a colorful bin of balls and started wagging her tail. Of course I picked the color, red and white stripes like a *Cat in the Hat* hat, but she chose the ball.

I let the ball sail through the air. It gets caught in a tree before it falls. This throws Sunny off for only a second as she doubles back to retrieve the ball. Then out of nowhere a crack of thunder seers through the air. I call to Sunny to come inside before we get poured on by the buckets that undoubtedly will dump rain on us soon, but I can't find her.

"Sunny!" I call again. "Sunny, come on, girl." I pick up the ball which sits in the middle of the yard. The thunder booms again. The sky looks ominous, like an expensive painting with streaks of grays and blacks and a shot of pink off in the distance, foreshadowing that sunny skies will follow this fast-moving storm. *"Sunny!"* This isn't fun anymore as the sky opens with a downpour. That's when I see Sunny in the far corner of the yard hiding behind a bush. I have to grab her weight with all my might to pull her toward the door. My older brother opens the back door and calls for Sunny to come get a treat. Even that doesn't make her budge. Together we pull her inside but not before we are both soaking wet.

Sunny doesn't even shake her coat like she does after Dad gives her a bath. She just stands in the kitchen quivering and cowering like she's been screamed at or something, but she hasn't been, of course. All we were doing was trying to get her to a dry place. One minute she is playing fetch having the time of her life. The next minute she's freaking out over a little thunderstorm.

"Mom, what is wrong with this dog? Doesn't she know the thunder and rain aren't going to hurt her?"

"Of course she doesn't know that, you weirdo. She's a dog!" says my brother. He's so obnoxious sometimes.

"Don't call your sister a name," says Mom, "and I'm not really sure why Sunny is acting this way. None of the dogs I had growing up ever acted this way during a storm, but I've heard that some dogs have trouble with storms, fireworks, and other loud sounds."

"Do you think she's being hurt? I mean, she's shaking and breathing hard. Look at all that drool." I point to the kitchen floor which is covered in a pool of drool below her mouth.

"I don't think so," says Mom, "but, I'll call the veterinarian just to be sure. Anyway, it looks like the storm is almost over." A light drizzle falls outside. The thunder is a faint sound now. Even the sun is peeking through the sky.

"I'm going to look for a rainbow," I say. "Call the vet, Mom."

*****

If you were the veterinarian, what would you do next? Make a list of Sunny's injuries. Then make a diagnostic (treatment) plan based upon the information that you have. When you are done, read what the veterinarian will do.

Name of the Animal (patient):

Type of Animal:

Symptoms or Injuries:

Treatment:

History:

*There is a history of Sunny reacting to a loud noise.

*The owner notes signs of drooling, panting, and shaking. She also is refusing to respond to basic commands. Her eyes are "bugged out."

*Sunny acts normal a short while after the noise has ended.

NOTE: With a detailed history, veterinarians and the clinic staff may be able to figure out what is wrong with a pet. A possible diagnosis of noise anxiety can be made in this case. Noise anxiety is the fear of noises such as thunder, fireworks, guns, or electronic devices.

Assessment:

*A full physical exam will help to rule out other potential causes of strange behavior. For example, pain or discomfort can make a dog shake and pant.

*In this case, Sunny is acting normal in the exam room, and the exam is unremarkable.

Treatment Plan:

*In the event of a storm or fireworks, create a comfort zone at home. Close all windows and blinds. Turn up a noise-making device that a pet is accustomed to. This could be music or a fan.

*Train a dog to focus her attention on games and treats.

*Act relaxed around your dog when she is anxious. Do not console your dog with speech or petting if she is exhibiting mild anxiety. This may encourage the fear behavior.

*Drugs can be prescribed if the anxiety is severe enough. There are a variety of medications a veterinarian can prescribe to make a pet feel better.

*Pheromone products for dogs may naturally help a dog relax.

*Products that wrap or snuggly fit around a pet's body may also be calming.

Noise anxiety is common. Dogs can't always understand where loud noises are coming from. Some dogs can get used to loud noises, though. If a dog used while hunting feared the noise of guns, the dog wouldn't be very helpful to the hunter.

*****

Sunny still doesn't love storms. She seems to sense when they are coming, too, long before we do. We try to make her as comfortable as possible. Mom bought a cool noise machine that sounds like a flowing river. When we know a storm is coming, we turn that machine up really loud and try to act normal with our activities. Unless there's a super big crack of thunder, she just sticks close to our sides. I think she knows that she is safe with us. I guess it's a good thing her name is Sunny. She seems to know that things always get better after a storm. The sun always comes out again!

Chocolate

The best part of summer vacation has finally arrived: the youth fair. Kids from all over the county will pour into town with their handiwork: hand-grown fruits and vegetables, crafted blankets and pillows, one-of-a-kind Lego creations, photographs, rock collections, and my favorite—homemade desserts. For those kids that don't feel like crafting, collecting, or baking, there's live animal pens where kids show off their cows, horses, and rabbits. You name it—almost any farm animal you can think of will be filling the barns at the county fair. Thousands of people will walk through those smelly barns in an attempt to see a baby pig or a milking cow. Then they'll make their way over to the craft building to see the homemade and homegrown creations of the area youth. Of course, that's only the beginning of a great day. Who can forget about the carnival rides, elephant ears, and corndogs on a stick?

This year I'm entering four things: the watermelon I grew in our garden (though I know it's not going to win as I've seen much larger), a collection of rocks I found along the shore of Lake Michigan and identified, a series of pictures featuring three robin eggs from when they were first found to when they hatched (so cool), and chocolate chip muffins with a special recipe I've been tinkering with for over a week. I can hardly wait to add to the ribbon collection as I know these muffins are going to score big.

Tutu comes barreling through the cat door from the basement and into the kitchen just as I'm setting out the ingredients for my muffins. Tutu doesn't understand that the cat door is designed for *cats*, like our cat Charge. The problem is that Charge thinks he's a dog, and Tutu thinks she's a cat. By size alone, you couldn't tell the difference between the two. Tutu is a teacup Yorkie, which means she's small enough to fit into a purse, or at least one of those travel bags you see celebrities carrying their dogs around in in Hollywood, but we are far from celebrities. We rescued Tutu from the animal shelter when her previous owner died and no one wanted her. From the first day we brought her home, she and Charge got along great. Charge retrieved sticks in the backyard that I'd throw for Tutu who preferred laying in the sun and licking herself. Yes, their roles are completely reversed, but they're happy. Who cares what visitors to our house might think? And at night, when they're curled on top of each other in Tutu's dog bed, you can't help but fall in love with them.

"I'm running to the store," says Dad. "Do you need anything for your muffins?" he asks.

"Nope, thanks. I think I have everything I need," I say.

"Going to tell me your super-secret special first place winning ingredient?" he asks.

"No way. If I tell you, then it won't be super-secret, and only super-secret will win me that first place ribbon." Dad rolls his eyes and smiles. I shoo him out of the kitchen and begin adding ingredients to the mixing bowl while I preheat the oven.

I can't find the mixer in its usual spot, so I go to the pantry to see if my baking-challenged mother has put it in there. It's a rare day when she makes the desserts in this family, and when she does she messes up my routine by putting everything back in the wrong place. I can't be mad at her, though. She's crafty with words. She's an author. Baker? *No way.*

Just as predicted, the mixer is hiding on the top shelf of the pantry behind the cereal. I have to get a chair to reach it. I hear trouble before I see it. A loud thud sends something to the floor in the kitchen. I grab the mixer and turn around in the kitchen to find the mixing bowl splattered all over the floor. A mess of sugar and eggs, flour and butter, vanilla and chocolate, smears the floor and the sides of the island cabinets. Looking none too innocent on top of the counter, is Charge. He stops to lick his paw while Tutu ravenously tries to eat as much as she can from the floor before I can get to the mess.

"Tutu, *no!*" With one hand I pick up Tutu and put her in the backyard. With the other hand I scoop up Charge and put him in the basement, locking the cat door. Dad will be back soon. I can't let him find this disaster.

I'm mopping up the last of the dry crumbs on the counter when he comes in with groceries. "Need a taste-tester?" Dad asks.

"I had a bit of a setback," I say. "I hope you bought more eggs."

"You said you had everything you needed."

39

"Yeah, that was before I had some helpers get in the way," I say, gesturing toward Tutu who sits outside the back door with sad eyes begging to be let back in. Charge is forgoing the sympathy card altogether by constantly batting at the cat door with his paw which is quite annoying.

"Did they eat anything?" asks Dad, whose face is turning red with worry.

"Sure they did. I'm sorry. I was in the pantry getting the mixer."

"What did they eat?"

"The usual stuff that goes into muffins, Dad, except I hadn't added the special ingredient yet."

"Did Tutu get any chocolate?" Dad is already reaching for the phone, anticipating my answer.

"Of course she did. You can't make chocolate chip muffins without cocoa power."

"Shut off the oven. You'll have to cook later. Don't take your eyes off that dog," he says, pointing to Tutu.

"Dad, what is wrong with Tutu?"

"I hope nothing yet, but chocolate is highly toxic, especially because she's so small. I'm calling the vet."

"Is she going to be okay?" Dad doesn't answer as he's already punching in the phone number. I go outside and pick up Tutu. She wags her tail as I pet her short fur. I close my eyes and say a silent prayer, a cooking disaster gone terribly wrong.

*****

If you were the veterinarian, what would you do next? Make a list of Tutu's injuries. Then make a diagnostic (treatment) plan based upon the information that you have. When you are done, read what the veterinarian will do. **NOTE:** This case is a bit different as Tutu is not yet showing alarming symptoms. However, Dad is concerned that Tutu may have eaten something harmful. Write what symptoms you think you might see in a dog that has ingested something harmful.

Name of the Animal (patient):

Type of Animal:

Symptoms or Injuries:

Treatment:

History:

*Tutu has a history of ingesting a toxic substance. This means she ate something that can harm her. In this case, that substance is chocolate.

*It is important for proper treatment to note when the toxic exposure occurred and how much of the toxic substance was ingested. This information will help guide the veterinarian with Tutu's treatment. Tutu ate chocolate within an hour of visiting the veterinarian. Cocoa powder and chocolate chips were ingredients in the muffin mix.

FACT: Chocolate is not toxic to humans. In fact, it is known to make certain veterinarians happy. Chocolate is dangerous to dogs because their bodies do not metabolize it well. This means dog's bodies have trouble digesting and handling chocolate.

Assessment:

*Tutu is currently acting normal. This is because she ate the chocolate within the last hour. The signs would be worse if more time has passed.

NOTE: Sometimes dogs will show severe signs after ingesting something toxic. If Tutu is not treated quickly, her signs could include vomiting, diarrhea, restlessness, heart problems, seizures, and even death.

*Other tests done to better assess Tutu are: temperature, heart rate and rhythm (how the heart is beating), and blood testing.

Treatment Plan:

*The veterinarian immediately induces emesis. This means she makes Tutu vomit. This is done to remove as much toxin from the stomach as possible.

*The veterinarian administers activated charcoal. This is a medication that will help absorb toxins still in the stomach and intestines.

*Tutu will remain hospitalized so the veterinarian can monitor and manage more severe signs if they occur.

FACTS:

*The darker chocolates are more dangerous to dogs. This is due to the amount of toxic substance in the chocolate. Dark chocolate is more dangerous than milk chocolate. Cocoa powder is particularly dangerous.

*The size of the dog will determine severity of signs. A chocolate bar may cause diarrhea in a Labrador retriever, but it may cause a seizure in a dog as small as Tutu.

*Due to chocolate availability, veterinarians see more chocolate ingestion cases around the holidays.

*Keep chocolate away from pets. However, your friendly veterinarian loves chocolate!

*****

Tutu stayed at the veterinarian's office overnight. She is doing great today. I am so glad Dad knew to check Tutu for a chance of chocolate toxicity. I shudder to think about what could have happened if I had been home alone and wouldn't have known what to do. Dad went grocery shopping last night to buy new eggs. My chocolate chip muffins are sitting in a secure container on the top pantry shelf far away from Tutu and Charge. When I win my blue ribbon at the county fair, I am giving it to Tutu. She has shown me that what's really important in life is the safety of my loved ones—two *and* four-footed.

Gross

"Be in the car in five minutes!" yells Dad from downstairs like I haven't heard him for the last fifteen minutes. I'm trying to be ready. It's not my fault my alarm clock didn't go off. My sister has a basketball tournament all day today. One could accuse me of dragging my heels because the last thing I want to do is spend my Saturday an hour away from home watching a bunch of high school girls dribble a basketball up and down a court in a hot gym with sweaty teenagers *everywhere*, but that's not why I'm late. With Mom away on a business trip, it's been my responsibility to take care of our cat Oscar. *Clean the litter box. Fill the food bowl. Change the water.* The last thing I have to do make sure Oscar's locked up in my parent's bathroom when we leave so he doesn't find too much trouble. He's been known to push food off the counter or sneak out a loose screen in the window. Just last week he went missing for a whole day before we heard him crying at the back door to be let in.

"Oscar!" I yell, matching my Dad's frustration. I look in all of his usual hiding spots: under the bed in my sister's room (because it's the most cluttered and easiest place to be concealed), behind the couch, on the top shelf of my parent's closet. I'm about to give up when I hear a noise (and not the kind of noise you want to hear when you're already fifteen minutes late). It sounds like Oscar is vomiting a hairball. *Ugh.* Dad is not going to be happy.

"Dad! Oscar's got a hairball!"

"Then clean it up and let's get going. Your sister is already in the car!" I follow the gagging sound into my room. *Just great.* I grab an old notebook to try and catch the hairball (meaning less clean up), but when Oscar is done, it's not a hairball my orange fourth grade science notebook is balancing. It's vomit: food, liquid, grossness. I wouldn't normally be too worried because most living things get sick from time to time, but this is the second time she's vomited in the last two days. That is *not* normal. Poor Oscar. I pick him up and cuddle him like a kitten, like I did for the first three months of his life, carrying him around like a baby. That was before he started getting sassy and clawing his way out of my grasp. He lets me hold him which is another sign that he's not feeling well. I hear the car horn from the driveway. I set Oscar down on a towel on the floor of my parent's bathroom and try to make a nest for him.

"It's okay, Oscar," I say. "We'll have the neighbor check on you." I pet his furry head and watch his sad eyes follow me out the door.

*****

Thankfully my sister lost the second game of the day in a double elimination tournament, so we're headed home before 3:30. I don't think I could have handled all the excitement of another game. *Not.* The phone rings in the car, jolting me awake in the backseat. My sister grumbles about the disturbance. My dad pushes the call accept button on the dashboard. The voice of our neighbor, Mr. Yerington, comes in loud and clear.

"Uh, I think we have a problem, Ed."

"What's wrong?" asks my dad.

"Well, I just checked on Oscar like you asked."

"Did he vomit again?"

"N…no. It's not the vomit. There's…well, Oscar seems to have worms, Ed."

That's the exact moment that I feel like vomiting myself.

When we get home, Mr. Yerington's assessment is proven accurate without a doubt. Oscar's litter box is crawling with white rice. Only white rice doesn't crawl. It doesn't even move, for that matter. My sister runs out of the room and straight into her bathroom the minute she lays eyes on the litter box. That's my first instinct, too, but then I look at Oscar, and I feel bad for him.

"Dad? Is Oscar going to be okay?"

"I think so," he says. "Make sure Oscar stays confined to this room. I'll make an appointment with the veterinarian."

*****

If you were the veterinarian, what would you do next? Make a list of Oscar's injuries. Then make a diagnostic (treatment) plan based upon the information that you have. When you are done, read what the veterinarian will do.

Name of the Animal (patient):

Type of Animal:

Symptoms or Injuries:

Treatment:

History:

*The owner noticed little white worms on Oscar's stool. (poop)

*Oscar will occasionally vomit a hairball. He vomited some liquid today.

*Oscar is acting normal otherwise.

*The owner states that Oscar is a 100% indoor cat. After further questioning by the veterinary team, it was learned that Oscar sometimes escapes to the outdoors.

Assessment:

*Small, dry, seed-like objects are seen stuck to the back of Oscar's legs. The veterinarian determines this to be dried tapeworm segments.

*Some dark debris is seen within the hair coat. The veterinarian identifies this debris as flea dirt. (poop)

FACT: Tapeworms are long, flat, segmented worms that live in the animal's intestine. The worm may be up to a foot long inside the pet. Pieces of the worm, described as segments, fall off of the worm and get passed out the rectum of the animal. The segments contain eggs. When the segments are fresh, they can move and stretch. When they are dried, the segments look like sesame seeds.

FACT: Flea dirt is flea poop. If you see this in a hair coat, you can identify a flea problem. Fleas bite an animal and pass the digested blood as this dark debris. To test if the dark debris is not just regular dirt, a veterinarian or technician will smash the dark pieces on a wet towel. If the pieces turn red, this confirms the debris is digested blood. (flea poop)

FACT: Tapeworms depend on fleas. The most common type of tapeworm found in pets spends part of its life inside a flea's body. While grooming, or cleaning itself, the pet eats a flea that contains the tapeworm. That is how the tapeworm gets established inside the pet. Keep your eyes peeled for fleas if you notice your pet has tapeworms.

Treatment Plan:

*The veterinarian will select the proper type of dewormer to clear the tapeworms from Oscar.

*The fleas must also be controlled or Oscar will keep getting infected with tapeworms.

NOTE: There are multiple types of tapeworms. Animals can get some of them by hunting. Humans and pets can also get tapeworms by eating under-cooked meat. Humans can get the type of tapeworm that Oscar had, but they would have to eat a flea.

*****

My sister is still being a brat. She won't hold Oscar yet, but I will. He's feeling so much better now that he's got medicine to take away the tapeworms and fleas. Mom made sure the house was clear and clean of fleas, though we never did spot any. Sometimes I guess you just don't know how an animal gets sick. All I know is that Oscar is lucky to have an owner like me that loves him through the nice *and* the yucky.

Bad Breath

There's nothing worse than spending spring break sick and in bed. My friends are off traveling the country—Disney World, a Bahamas cruise, a beach house along Lake Michigan. Even my friend who is driving ten hours to see family in Rhode Island has it better than I do. Flipping the channel on the television remote for the tenth time in the last ten minutes, I settle back into my pillow and try to get comfortable watching some old dinosaur movie from the 1990s.

"I'm going to the store for some groceries and cough medicine," says Mom from the doorway of my room. "Anything special you want?" She gives me a dopey *I feel sorry for you* kind of smile. Even though I'm too old to be babied by my mom, it still makes me feel special.

"How about that magic medicine that will simultaneously take away this virus and transport us to a tropical beach after only two doses?"

"I think they might be out of that medicine at the pharmacy," says Mom. "I'll check the magic store." There's that smile again. "Hang in there. As my grandmother used to say, *this too shall pass.*"

I turn back to the television and the crabby mood I've put myself in for the day. As soon as Mom leaves, our dog CJ jumps on the bed and nestles into the pool of blankets at my feet since I'm sweating like...well, like a dog. CJ is older than I am. My parents say he's their first baby. It's funny, though, that no one seems to remember what the *C* and *J* even stand for. I like to think CJ stands for *Crazy Joe* because unless you get close enough to see the graying of his nose and ears, you'd think he was still a pup the way he jumps around like crazy. But today CJ is hanging with me, and I'm grateful.

My stomach is growling as I settle on a cooking show on the television, one of those far out stations that you don't usually have the patience to scan all the way to. It's a competition show. Everyone is making something with eggs. CJ turns around in a circle before readjusting himself in my comforter. Crazy Joe is at it again.

"Come here, boy," I say. Without hesitation, CJ walks over to me and plops himself against my side. I must miss my friends pretty badly to be talking to my dog. As if reading my mind, CJ jerks up his head and plants a giant kiss on my neck. "Seriously?" I wipe the slobber but can't stay mad at this adorable face. Then he does it again, this time getting my nose. "Oh my gosh, *what* have you been eating?" I push CJ away and roll over on my side and cry myself to sleep.

A gentle tug on my arm startles me awake. "Hey," whispers Mom. "I brought you some more medicine."

"Thanks," I say.

"I see you have company." She tousles CJ's fur. He responds by drooling over my stomach.

"Mom, has CJ's breath always smelled this bad?"

"I know what you mean. It seems to be getting worse."

"Can't you brush his teeth or something? Plus, his teeth look pretty dark in the back." I point to the uneven markings on his teeth as he drools over my bed.

"I've heard of that. I think the veterinarian's even mentioned it before. CJ has his wellness visit tomorrow. I'll ask, okay? In the meantime, take your medicine, and get some rest."

"This has been the worst spring break ever," I say.

"Yeah, I know, but think of all the quality time you are getting with CJ and me. When your dad's home, maybe you'll feel up to playing a board game."

"*A board game?*" I roll my eyes.

"You can't criticize something you haven't tried."

I sigh because I know she's right and because she's trying very hard to make me happy.

*****

If you were the veterinarian, what would you do next? Make a list of CJ's injuries. Then make a diagnostic (treatment) plan based upon the information that you have. When you are done, read what the veterinarian will do.

Name of the Animal (patient):

Type of Animal:

Symptoms or Injuries:

Treatment:

History:

*CJ has bad breath. This condition is called halitosis.

*There are several possible causes of CJ's bad breath:

1. Dental disease: This is the most common cause of bad breath in pets. Dogs can develop plaque and tartar. Plaque forms when very small organisms (bacteria) grow in the saliva and around the teeth. When dental plaque becomes hard or mineralized, tartar forms. The plaque and tartar play a role in cavities, tooth decay, and gum disease. Severe dental disease may be indicated if a pet is pawing at the mouth, drooling, dropping food when eating, or if loose teeth are seen.

2. Lip fold infection: Some dogs have extra skin on the muzzle. This skin can create a fold that collects saliva. This warm skin fold is a great place to grow some stinky bacteria.

3. More severe problems: Bad breath may indicate a more serious problem with the kidneys, liver, lungs, or digestive system. If a veterinarian suspects such an underlying problem, blood work, urinalysis (pee testing), and other tests will be needed.

Assessment:

*Most cat and dog mouths can be assessed by a veterinarian initially without anesthesia. Anesthesia is a controlled sleeping state a veterinarian can create with drugs and devices that produce medical gas mixtures. **NOTE:** People can get bitten attempting to look in their pet's mouth. Ask an adult if you think your pet's mouth should be examined. It may be best if a veterinarian or veterinarian technician examines your pet's mouth.

*During the exam, a veterinarian looks for gum inflammation (red gums), tartar, teeth that move, damaged or broken teeth, and tumors (a bump or growth of tissue).

*To closely examine the teeth and mouth, anesthesia and possible X-rays of the mouth will be needed. The veterinarian will use a metal instrument to probe the space between the teeth and gums. This helps the veterinarian to determine how healthy the teeth and gums are.

Treatment Plan:

*The veterinarian diagnoses dental disease. A professional dental cleaning and assessment is recommended.

1. Tartar is removed with special instruments above and below the gum line.

2. The teeth and gums are closely examined.

3. The teeth are polished.

4. Possibly dental X-rays will be taken.

*Home care will be discussed with the owner.

*Tooth brushing is recommended to remove plaque and bacteria.

*DO NOT use human toothpaste. This will upset the pet's stomach. Use pet toothpaste flavored with chicken, beef, or other pet flavors.

*Do not worry about reaching the inner surfaces of the pet's teeth. Tartar and plaque tend to form mostly on the outer surface of dog and cat teeth.

*BE CAREFUL. Do not brush if your pet is scared. Work with an adult to introduce the process very gradually.

*Dental treats will be recommended.

*Some treats have been proven in experiments to prevent plaque and dental disease. Look for a VOHC symbol on treats or foods. (VOHC stands for the Veterinary Oral Health Council.)

*Firm things to chew may be recommended.

*Be careful of objects harder than teeth. Dogs can fracture teeth when chewing on hard objects. The damaged teeth may cause pain or infection. The fractured or broken teeth may then need to be removed from your pet's mouth by a veterinarian.

FACT: Humans have 32 adult teeth. Dogs have 42. Cats have 30.

FACT: Most puppies and kittens start to lose their "baby" teeth when they are 16 weeks of age. Children tend to start losing teeth around age 6 or 7 years. Puppies and kittens usually have all of their adult teeth in place by 6 months old!

*****

"Why do you look so sad?" asks Mom.

I am sitting outside in the backyard. She hands me a glass of lemonade. "Thanks," I say, taking the lemonade. "I don't want spring break to end."

"I thought you said this was the worst spring break ever," says Mom, sitting in a lawn chair across from me.

"Well, it started out pretty rough, but I feel a whole lot better now. Plus, CJ is going to miss me being gone."

"He's not so difficult to be around now that he has a fresh mouth," says Mom.

As if on cue, CJ reaches toward my face with his slimy tongue and plants a big kiss on my cheek. It still feels gross, but at least I am not gagging from the smell.

"He's so much easier to be around," I say. "But maybe it's time for you to brush his teeth again—just to keep it that way!"

Mystery

Mom hands my brother and I our annual Christmas ornament. It's a tradition she started even before we understood what Christmas was. Her parents did the same thing for her. When she married my dad, Grandma gave her all the ornaments from her youth. It's kind of cool to look at all of her old ornaments on the tree. Each year our ornament represents something that we did or somewhere we went—our Mickey Mouse ornament from the year we went to Disney World, a baseball bat ornament for my first year in little league, and a racecar ornament from the year I won the district championship for the Cub Scouts' car race.

Dad is holding up his phone, another tradition to record our unwrapping of the new ornaments. My little brother and I unwrap our ornaments at the same time, trying to be extra careful because one year our ornaments were glass balls with a picture of Mount Rushmore. I was so excited that I let the ornament slip out of my hand. It shattered to the floor breaking into a hundred pieces. My mom cried.

"Chicago Cubs!" my brother yells.

"World Series champs!" I add. "Cool pick, Mom. Thanks." We've all been living in disbelief since early November when the Cubs won the World Series—after 108 years. The Wrigley Field sign declaring the Cubs as *World Series Champions* makes for a pretty cool ornament. I hang my ornament in a prominent spot on the tree, right at the top where everyone will see it.

When we are done decorating, Mom takes out a new box of tinsel, a shiny, silvery decoration that looks like narrow strips of icicles hanging from the tree. When I was little I used to get mad at Mom for not letting me help put the tinsel on the tree. Now I know that it's something that makes her really happy to do alone, so I don't complain. I know that neither my brother nor I are patient enough to place the tinsel as perfectly as she does. Instead we put Mom's collectable snowmen around the house, filling every possible open space.

Wrigley, our new kitten, follows behind us while nipping at our legs. She showed up on our doorstep the day after the Cubs won the World Series. It's a true story. We put signs up around the neighborhood, but no one claimed her. And even though she's a girl, Dad and Mom let us call her Wrigley. It seemed like a fitting name since that's the home of the Cubs. She's sweet—when she's asleep. Otherwise, she's a feisty little thing. I am finding Lego pieces all over my room that she's dug out of my Lego box. Today she's enjoying knocking over the snowmen we are putting out. I know she'll settle down like our old cat Larry did, but I have forgotten how annoying the kitten stage can be.

Mom helps us put up the rest of the decorations from the Christmas box. We aren't allowed back into the living room with the Christmas tree until it's dark enough to see the tree at night—another tradition. If it's one thing we all know in this family, it's that you'd better let Mom get all of her tradition in or she's one cranky lady. But she has to keep running into the living room to yell at Wrigley. Every time we hear a jingling sound we know that Wrigley has climbed into the tree again. Mom is getting highly annoyed. Finally she scoops the cat up and banishes her to the basement, locking the cat door that will prevent her from getting to the living room. Poor naughty Wrigley looks so sad staring through the cat door.

At precisely *dark enough*, in Mom's words, she lets Dad, my brother, and me into the living room. The tree sure is stunning, from the lights to the tinsel to the two new perfectly-placed Wrigley Field ornaments. It is truly a magical thing to have a World Series ornament on *our* tree. Who could ever have imagined such a thing?

*****

After a good night's sleep where I dream about all the things I want for Christmas, the day starts with a bang.

"Get your Mom!" yells Dad. He's standing in the hallway. Wrigley runs past my dad and into the basement as my dad tries to chase her.

"What happened?" I ask. But I see the answer before Dad speaks. "You or the cat?" I ask, spying the vomit on the hallway floor.

"Not funny!" says Dad.

I thought it was a good joke, but I don't tell my Dad that. Instead I get my Mom. "What? That's the third time Wrigley has thrown up this morning. What is wrong with that cat?" She sighs as she follows me to my dad who is cleaning up the vomit. "Find Wrigley," she says to me.

I open the basement door. It takes me a while to find her. She is hiding behind cardboard boxes in the back of the basement. "What's the matter, Wrigley? Do you have a tummy ache?"

She doesn't purr in answer. I pet her back and under her chin. No purring. She seems sad, just lying there staring into space. I pick her up. She doesn't try to fight me like she usually does.

When she and I get upstairs, Mom offers Wrigley some sips of water from her bowl, but she doesn't want to drink. "I think we should take Wrigley to the vet," Mom says to Dad. "She hasn't been doing much today but lying around—more than usual. Is there food left in her food bowl?"

I get up to check. "Her bowl is still full," I say.

"She is not acting normally," says Mom. "Put Wrigley into her cat bed. I'll call the doctor for an appointment."

*****

If you were the veterinarian, what would you do next? Make a list of Wrigley's injuries. Then make a diagnostic (treatment) plan based upon the information that you have. When you are done, read what the veterinarian will do.

Name of the Animal (patient):

Type of Animal:

Symptoms or Injuries:

Treatment:

History:

*Wrigley is acting sick. She has been vomiting, she is not eating her food, and she is lethargic. She has no energy and wants to sleep all the time. Most cats will sleep a good portion of the day, but Wrigley has not gotten up to greet the owner or eat a treat. This is a tremendous change from earlier in the week when, as if excited by the holiday season, Wrigley had been very energetic playing around the Christmas tree.

Assessment:

Physical exam:

*Wrigley is dehydrated. In other words, her body lost a large amount of water through vomiting. Also, Wrigley has been unable to drink water to account for that loss. If an animal does not drink enough water to account for any losses, it can become very sick. Severe dehydration can even lead to death. The veterinarian can detect dehydration in multiple ways.

1. The skin loses its normal elasticity or tents up. This is what a veterinarian is testing for when she pinches your pet's skin. When a pet is dehydrated, the skin does not go back immediately into place.

2. The eyes of the animal may appear sunken in.

3. The gums may be sticky due to a lack of moisture.

*During the physical exam, the veterinarian also feels the abdomen. A veterinarian does this to check for organ (liver, spleen, urinary bladder, kidneys, and intestines) enlargement. Tumors, or masses, may sometimes be detected this way. As the veterinarian palpates Wrigley's abdomen, she thinks an area of intestines seems bunched up.

*No other physical exam abnormalities are noted while examining Wrigley. The veterinarian examines the mouth carefully. The eyes, ears, and hair coat are examined. The lymph nodes are normal in size. Lymph nodes are small organs located in various locations. These nodes are important for an immune system to protect a body. When the lymph nodes are enlarged, it could indicate infection or cancer.

*The veterinarian recommends blood work. Hypokalemia is detected. This means Wrigley has low potassium. One way potassium can be lost is when an animal vomits frequently. Potassium is important for muscles to work properly. Since the heart is a big muscle, low potassium can be very serious. Azotemia is detected. This means high levels of certain compounds are found that indicate dehydration.

*Abdominal radiographs are done. (X-rays). X-rays are beams of energy used to make a picture of objects inside a body. Wrigley's X-ray pictures show abnormal findings. The intestines have a collection of air bubbles that could indicate they are bunched together.

Diagnosis:

*At this time, the veterinarian is suspicious of a linear foreign body. This could be a string, thread, or other long object that gets stuck and then binds up the intestines. Normal digesting food is unable to pass the obstruction that is formed. More damage can be caused as the intestines attempt to move in their usual way. The linear object can cut into the intestinal wall and form a hole. This can cause a life-threatening abdominal infection.

Treatment Plan:

*The dehydration and potassium losses should be corrected. This involves the veterinary team placing an intravenous catheter. The port placed into the vein will help the team administer fluids with added potassium.

*Abdominal exploratory surgery is performed. With the aid of anesthesia (Medications are given to create a sleeping, pain-free state.), the veterinarian will open the abdomen surgically. The entire digestive tract needs to be examined. For example, strings can get caught around a tongue or get hung up in the stomach. The veterinarian identifies the area of bunched-up intestine. Then the intestine is cut to remove the linear object. The object is identified as Christmas tree *icicles*, or a foil-like plastic form of tinsel.

NOTE: Christmas decorations can be dangerous for dogs and cats. They can be attracted to the shiny materials used in the decorations.

Wrigley was lucky that the linear material did not cut through and damage her intestines. If this happened, the veterinarian may have had to remove sections of Wrigley's intestine. Delaying the surgery may have increased the risk for more damage to occur.

*****

I don't care what I have waiting under the tree this year. I already got an early present when the veterinarian found that tinsel inside Wrigley and saved her life. She's back to her normal, crazy, naughty self. That makes me happier than any present possibly could. Mom took all of the tinsel off the tree as soon as she knew that Wrigley had eaten a piece. I know she's going to be sad because she has to change her tradition. But it's okay. Now we have a new tradition to celebrate—the Chicago Cubs winning the World Series every year!

Dr. Ed Blesy graduated from the University of Illinois College of Veterinary Medicine in 1997. In 2006 he opened his own clinic, St. Joseph Animal Wellness Clinic, in Southwest Michigan. He has appeared on-air with Wild Bill on 97.5FM radio to answer listeners' vet questions and written pet-related articles for *Lakeside Family Magazine*. He and his wife Marcy enjoy spending time on the beautiful beaches of Lake Michigan and attending the activities of their two sons.

Marcy Blesy is the author of several middle grade and young adult novels. Her picture book, *Am I Like My Daddy?*, helps children who experienced the loss of a parent when they were much younger. She has also been published in two *Chicken Soup for the Soul* books as well as various newspapers and magazines. By day she runs an elementary school library and enjoys spending time with her husband Ed and two boys.

Follow our *Be the Vet* Facebook page for more specific information.

We would love an Amazon review as well. Readers value the input of fellow readers.

Other Children's Books by Marcy Blesy:

Evie and the Volunteers Series

Join ten-year-old Evie and her friends as they volunteer all over town meeting lots of cool people and getting into just a little bit of trouble. There is no place left untouched by their presence, and what they get from the people they meet is greater than any amount of money.

Book 1   Animal Shelter

Book 2   Nursing Home

Book 3   After-School Program

Book 4   Food Pantry

Book 5: Coming Spring 2017